AF472500

Dedication

I dedicate this book to my dogs.

Table of Contents

Introduction

Chapter 1

Summer break was over. It was my sophomore year at West Coast high School. My name is Camryn Blu. I Live in California. I have light brown hair (almost blonde), green eyes and very tan. I have lived in Cali for about 2 years. I'm originally from NY City. My mom and dad both died when I was only 7 year old. I never knew why. I have always lived with my aunt Alyssa and My uncle John. My best friend is Kate. Im sitting in Social Studies. I've always hated that class. When I get home i'm going to go surf. The bell finally rings and I got to my advanced math class with all the nerds. I got put into this class because I catch along quick and everything is just easy to me. I've always really liked school too. I start to copy the notes in my journal about the new math material we are learning. The bell rings and I go to my locker and grab my stuff. I grab my backpack and all my books to go home.

After school I went straight home. I found my wet suit and pulled my hair into a Dutch

Braid and took off all my makeup, so I did not look like a zombie while I was surfing the waves. I would invite Kate but she is really scared of sharks or she is scared she will die. I decide to bring Lucky because she loves the water. Belmont Shore, is a dog friendly place. The beach is about a 10 minute ride from my house. I get in my jeep, and turn on the Bluetooth and start to sing along with the music playing.

The next thing I know I'm at Belmont Shore. I get my surfboard and let lucky out the car.

I walk over to spot where I lay my bag and towel down onto the sand. I grab lucky's ball and throw it into the water for her to fetch. I get my surfboard and walk over to the water. I step in with my black wetsuit and swim out to wait for a wave. There was a lot of surfers out here today. I have never seen a shark attack or even seen a shark before, so i'm not scared of anything. I wait for a good wave. Finally one comes, I get on my stomach and wait for it to come. Right while it is pushing me I stand up on my board. I love the beachy air and water splashing in my face, this is what I live for.

I finally wipe out and go back out for another wave. Some guys were all hanging out around that area too. We all talking and waiting for a wave to come. "So what school do you go to?" asked one of the guys. "I go to west coast high" I said.

There was a moment of silence. Then the next thing I heard was a scream from one of the boys. I look over and he is pulled under the water. The only thing that came to mind was shark. I had to get out of there, but I couldn't just leave him. I swam over to where is surfboard lays. I grab what is left of his arm, as he comes to the surface of the water.

I pull him onto my surfboard. I see the shark coming, so I kick it into the nose and it swims away.

I walk over to spot where I lay my bag and towel down onto the sand. I tell someone to call 911. I lay him down. He is screaming and crying. I put my arm on his stomach where is was also bitten. I try to stop the blood, but it stops on its own. My hands. They are healing him... I get up and run. I don't know what to do. My hands were healing him. I don't know how. It just closed up the wounds and stopped the bleeding. I call for lucky, and she comes running. I open the door for her and close it shut. I get in my jeep and go straight home. During my drive home I had like a vision-- I woke up around 9:00 today because all i could think about was how Kate and her family were going to try to kill me today. Still in my pj's I walked down stairs to tell Aunt Alyssa and Uncle John about it. When I walked down they were no place to be seen. Lucky was down stairs whimpering like something was wrong. I walked up to Lucky and started to pet her.

"What is wrong Lucky girl?"

She just kept on whimpering. I tried to call Aunt Alyssa and Uncle John but they did not answer my call. I started to call Jozie's name,

"Jozie, I need your help. Where is Aunt Alyssa and Uncle John?"

I said it about a few times. No response. After I said it a few more times, Jozie appear.

"Cam"

"Ya."

"Kate and her family have Aunt Alyssa and Uncle John. You have to go there right now and fight them both."

"How I'm not ready. Jozie. I am really scared..."

"It is okay. I have contacted people just like you. Who came from Galaxis. Plus, I will be helping you too Cam. We got this." of vision. That was wired... I pulled into the driveway, then I woke up around 9:00 today because all i could think about was how Kate and her family were going to try to kill me today. Still in my pj's I walked down stairs to tell Aunt Alyssa and Uncle John about it. When I walked down they were no place to be seen.

Lucky was down stairs whimpering like something was wrong. I walked up to Lucky and started to pet her.

“What is wrong Lucky girl?”

She just kept on whimpering. I tried to call Aunt Alyssa and Uncle John but they did not answer my call. I started to call Jozie's name,

“Jozie, I need your help. Where is Aunt Alyssa and Uncle John?” I said it about a few times. No response. After I said it a few more times, Jozie appear.

“Cam”

“Ya...”

“Kate and her family have Aunt Alyssa and Uncle John. You have to go there right now and fight them both.”

“How I’m not ready. Jozie. I am really scared...”

“It is okay. I have contacted people just like you. Who came from Galaxis. Plus, I will be helping you too Cam. We got this.”-- End of vision. That was wired... I pulled into the driveway,

Chapter 2

When I get home my aunt is staring at the tv. "What's going on Aunt Alyssa". I said

"Look Camryn, you're on tv" she says.

"Why are my hands healing him?" I say

"Their your powers, Cam"

"Powers? That's not true there is no such thing."

"Yes there is Camryn, your mom and dad both had powers"

"Huh. How is this even possible?"

"Cam I want you to listen to me, you may not believe me but just listen, please. You are not from earth. You're a Frosted that is what they call people like when you first get healing as your power. You are from a Planet called Galaxis. Spectralmask took over your planet when you were 6 years old. Your parents died from them. They are looking for people from Galaxis. They are trying to find you, (and people like you) so they can take your powers and kill you. That's how your mom and dad died. They were not strong enough to kill them. I promised your mom that I wouldn't tell you until your powers started to develop. This will take a while, about of month just to get powers all developed. I know you probably have lots more questions, but just go to bed now and we will talk about it in the morning. Uncle John and I need to find a way to delete this off the internet."

"Okay" I said. I walked up stairs to my room and pulled out my computer. I was trying to search for things that were related to the powers I have but there was nothing. I couldn't sleep that night. I was still so surprised about the whole thing. I'm still not sure if i believed it. I decided to Face Time Kate, and tell her about everything that happened today and that I have some sort of "powers" and there are monsters after me. I tried to Facetime her but she told me just to text her. I texted her this long paragraph about everything. A few minutes passed then a girl around 19 or 20 years of age showed up. "You shouldn't have told her any of that stuff Cam." She said

"What? I'm confused. Umm, who are you?" I said

"My name is Jozie. I need to tell you important stuff. Ok? Just listen." She said.

Jozie started to tell me about my past and what happened and how Kate (a Spectralmask) was after me. I was very worried that Kate was going to try to kill me. Jozie told me that she was one of the most powerful people here. I needed to tell Aunt Alyssa about Jozie and what she had told me. Also, surely she knew what to do. I was going to watch Netflix with my best friend Kate.

She was going to come over tonight. I needed to find a way to tell her not to come. We usually talk about things and eat our favorite ice cream. I have told Kate about everything. All my powers and the people coming for me. She knows about all my weaknesses and things I can do. I have trusted Kate all these years, but now I know it was all fake. That is why it has been so weird talking to her, she has been wanting to know everything I know. I knew I should've stopped talking about it when she was asking me. This was still all new to me to. I am very scared now. She had been lying to me all this time about who she really is. I still couldn't sleep so I Decided to go to starbucks. I grabbed my wallet and went out my window. Starbucks was about to close, but I made it their just in time.

I ordered my drink (Unsweetened Green Tea) and some food, (Chocolate Croissant) then payed. I waited there for a few minutes and started walking home.

While I was walking home something strange started happening. My hands started to tingle and the next thing I know I'm holding a car up with my hand. I started to run. It was so cold when my Tea flew all over me. But then I started to go invisible too. I keep going in and out of invisibility. Great. Another one of my powers. I needed to get home fast, to Aunt Alyssa.

Chapter 3

I finally made it back home. I told Aunt Alyssa everything. She said don't worry about and just go get some sleep you have school tomorrow. My head was pounding then I had a flashback of me first getting my power.

I woke up around 7 that morning because i had school. I really did not want to go. I was scared I would see all the Juniors I saw yesterday. I went into my bathroom and took off my Tea stained shirt because i dint feel like changing and took a hot shower. I washed all the salt water, and sand out of my hair from yesterday. I got out of my warm shower and grabbed my towels so I could dry off. I went back into my room and sat in front of my big mirror and blowed dryed my hair. Today was Friday. So I was going to invite Kate over, like what we usually do every Friday. Once I finished my blow drying my hair i plugged my straightener in and straightened my hair. I just left my hair flow down my back. I put on some mascara, blush and some nude lipstick and called it a day. I put on my Victoria secret pink shirts with some skinny jeans. I put on white converse and go downstairs to the kitchen.

I get some Greek yogurt and put some strawberries and raspberries and blackberries. I grab a spoon from the draw and sit at the table. I look throw my Instagram feed and look to see if anybody's said anything. I'm very surprised, but i don't see anything about the shark attack our about me saving Brad's life. It was about 9:00 a.m. when I finished. School started at 10:00. I decided to work on my projects and homework. I finish my math homework and one page of an essay. It was now 9:30. I usually left around 9:45. But since i had nothing to really do I grabbed my backpack and all of my text books and left. When i got there, I saw the surfer guys.

Once I parked I tried to ignore Brad as much as u could but I couldn't. He walked right beside me where i was walking

"Hi Camryn" Brad said

"Hey, how are you?" I said

"Good, what about you?"

"Fine." I say

"Okay well see you around. You should come surfing again today after school." Says brad

"Maybe" I say.

The bell rings and I Walk to my locker and open it up. I put the stuff i don't need into my locker and head to English class. I walked into it like I would any other day. I didn't notice anybody, starting or looking at me. Mrs. Sunny started teaching her lesson over Punctuation. I leaned on my forearm and my eyes closed. The next thing I know, the bell rings and it is time for 2nd, science...

I skip through school really fast. I'm still thinking about if i should go surfing. It was a bit cloudy today, I think it was going to rain and I have homework and Kate and I got to hang out too. When i was driving home, I stopped at the stop light and that whole squad of boys pulled up. I tried to look away but they were calling my name.

"Oh. Hi guys" I said

"Hey cam!" said Ty

"So, what you guys doing?"

"Going to go surf after we change, you coming?" said Luke

" OH, I don't know" I said

"Please come. Everybody says the waves our great today because of the storm coming! Hurry so we can get done before the storm Cam!" Said Brad.

"Okay maybe" I said.

The light turns green before I knew it. I guess I would come with them for a little. How bad could it be?

Chapter 4

I went home and grabbed my stuff for another day at the beach. but instead of having to grab anything. I was trying to see if i had another one of my powers and i did. I was able to lift things up without even grabbing anything with my hands. It floated up. I pulled it close to me and it worked! I was able to do everything, without touching it. Just using my powers. Kate texted me and said she was going out to dinner tonight with Josh, her boy friend. She invited me to come to. She said she would pick me up at 7:30. I agreed and

went up stairs and slipped on my wetsuit. I put my hair into a messy bun and I went downstairs and decided to make myself something to eat. I decided to make myself a sandwich with some strawberries on the side and without using any of my powers. I opened the pantry and took out the bread. Then, i opened the fridge with a soft swift and took out ham and cheese with the strawberries on the side. I forgot i needed to take off my make up to so I walked upstairs and took it off.

Once i was ready to leave, I opened the door and called for lucky to come to. I grabbed my surfboard and the leash for lucky. Lucky came running. I lifted her up with my powers and put her in the car. I plugged my phone in with the AUX cord because it was almost dead and listened to some music on my way to the beach.

When i got there the whole squad full of boys were already there, out in the ocean surfing the waves. I found a spot to lay down my stuff and got the ball for lucky and threw it into the blue, deep waters of the ocean. I got my surfboard and went into the ocean. I went over to where the squad of boys were hanging out.

"Hey guys!" I said.

"Oh hey Cam, I didn't think you were going to come today" Said brad.

"Well I came, so ready to catch some waves today?" I said.

"Ya" Said Luke.

Lucky came swimming by me so i could throw the ball. I picked up the ball, making sure i actually used my hands this time and threw it closer to shore this time.

"Is that your dog?" Said Ty

" Ya, her name is Lucky" I said.

We must of all seen the big wave coming because we all layed down on our boards.

"I bet you Brad will be the first one to wipe out" Ty said.

"Ya maybe, but for sure I will be the last to wipe out" I said with some sass and a grin on my face.

We all stood up on our board and surfed the wave. Brad was the first one to wipe out. This one curved around and I got out of the tunnel, everyone else wiped out. I finally wiped out, and everybody was clapping for me and cheering for me. I don't know why though, I have done that before. The squad of boys came over.

"Cam that was amazing, how did you stay on so long, like we have never seen a girl stay on like that? That was just, like whoa, we all wiped out under the tunnel." Said Luke.

"Oh well, I don't know. I was just keeping balance and I stayed on and went through the tunnel" I said.

They all looked at me in disbelief. I walked over to my stuff and called for Lucky to come to me. Lucky came pouncing over with the ball in her mouth. The squad of guys came over.

"Where you going cam?" Said Brad.

"I really have to go, my friend is coming soon, and I'm not ready yet, we are going out to dinner with her boyfriend." I said.

"Oh well, have fun Cam, see you later" Said Luke.

I walked away over to my jeep with Lucky by my side. I had just realized Micah wasn't with them today. I wonder if had to do something. I pulled into my driveway and took Lucky out of my car and went up to my room. It was almost 6:00 and Kate and Josh will be picking me up at 7:30. I went upstairs and took a shower. When I got out it was 6:23. I walked into my room and grabbed the blow dryer and blew my hair dry and let it my natural hair flow and put on some natural makeup. I put on some shorts with a black crop top with a cream colored cardigan.

Beep, Beep. I heard Josh's car outside my house. I walked outside and locked the door on the way out. When i walked over I was really surprised to see Micah in the car to. I opened the door and sat in the back with Micah.

“Hi Micah, Hey Kate and Josh” I said with a grin on my face.

“Hey Camryn” Said Micah and Kate at the same time.

“Since you were going to be alone tonight, I told Josh to bring a friend with him” said Kate.

“Oh cool.” I said

“So how is everyone today?” said Micah

“Good, what about you?” Said Kate

“I'm fine” Said Micah

“Where were you today, we all went surfing and i thought you were going to be there to, you were in the car with them?”

“I had to do homework, and get ready…” he said.

“Oh” I said

The drive was short to the place we were eating. It was called Lawry's The Prime Rib. We sat down in the back. I was sitting next to Micah while Kate and Josh sat next to each other Our waiter came in about 3 minutes. It was a boy. But just not any boy. It was Ty, taking our order.

“Oh hi Cam” Ty said.

“Hi” I said back.

“I dint know you and Micah were dating” He said

At the same time we both said “We are not dating”

“Oh, well what I can get you to drink?” he said

“I would like some water please” I said

“Coke” Josh said

“Ice tea” Kate said

“Ice tea, please” Said Micah

We all carried onto our night, talking and eating our delicious steaks. It was around 9 when we finally got our bill. We all got into the car still talking about things that were just random. I still haven't told Kate about the whole powers thing. We all went to Kate’s house and watched some Netflix. I didn’t sit by Micah. I sat on the end by Kate. We decided to watch the movie The Conjuring. The whole time I was watching it, I was really jumpy.

Some points in the movie i wished Micah was sitting by me. No i don’t like him, but just as a friend. He hasn't brought up the shark attack, actually nobody has surprisingly.

I kept seeing Micah looking at me out of the corner of his eye to. I felt bad that i wasn't sitting next to him in this movie that was really scary. I decided to get up and get some ice cream for everybody. When I came back to the couch, I gave everybody a spoon and their ice cream. But instead of sitting next to Kate I sat by Micah. We watched the rest of the movie. It was about 11:30 at night and i had josh drive me home. When I got home Aunt Alyssa and Uncle John were sleeping in bed. In the morning i needed to tell her about my new power. I went upstairs and took a hot shower. I slipped on some pj’s and called it a night.

Chapter 5

Next morning, I woke up around 10 ish and went downstairs for breakfast. Aunt Alyssa was cooking breakfast for everyone. She was making eggs and biscuits with bacon. I went to the Coffee maker and made me some coffee. Uncle John must have gone to work already, because he was nowhere to be seen. I sat down on the couch and put on my favorite show, Scream Queens.

"Aunt Alyssa" I said

"Ya sweetie?"

"I think I have a new power I discovered yesterday."

"Oh, what is it?"

"I can move things without touching them with my hands"

"That is good! Know you can, even more be more powerful than ever. The more powers that you get, the better it will be if you ever face a Spectralmask you can defeat them."

"Oh well I guess that is good"

"Ya it really is"

Aunt Alyssa finished cooking breakfast for the both of us. We sat at the table watching Scream Queens. I loved how Chanel Is rude to the other Channels, it's just so funny. I texted Kate to come over, because I wanted her to know about everything, the whole powers thing and being from another world called Galaxis and how Spectralmask are after me and I cannot let them know all my weaknesses. The next thing I know Kate is over to my house.

"So Cam, what did you need to talk about"

"First of, this may sound really crazy, but just believe me, trust me on this okay?"

"Okay Cam I trust you and believe you."

"Okay well, I'm from a planet called Galaxis. I have these powers that, our very ordinary, that nobody could dream of having. There are these things called Spectralmask, they are after me. I cannot let them know my weaknesses or anything about me"

"okay, what are your weaknesses?"

" well i'm terrified of seeing on.

Page 19

I have not developed all my powers, and I do not know what they look like.

" Okay, well I must be going know, I have to go do some things for my parents" She said with a smirk on her face.

" Okay bye Kate see you tomorrow?"

I just went and hung out at the beach today. When i got home it was around 6 and j decided to go to bed earlier. I fell asleep around 8. I had a dream about how i was going to fight them soon. I woke up. I walked down stairs. Aunt Alyssa was sitting on the couch. She look very scared.

"Cam they are here. They are in Beverly Hills, you have to fight them."

" But I don't know if i'm ready." I said.

" It' okay, me and Uncle John will help you prepare if you ever see one."

" Ok"

I walked up stairs and took a long shower. Thinking about the Spectralsk, and if it will be hard to fight against them or easy. If i'm stronger than them. What they look like. I get out of the shower and blow dry my hair. I put on some Pj's. I hear a weird voice. Jozie showed up again. She started to tell me everything she told me before.

"Hello? Is anybody there?:

No response. I hear a soft whisper in the wind. I think it saying Cameryn or maybe hi.

"Hello?"

I see a shadow in my room. I think i should run but i'm curious what it was.

"Um, hello?"

The shadow appears. It's Jozie.

" Hi Cameron"

"Hey jozie"

" OK well Cam, I have something you should know right away."

" Ok well what is it."

" It is about your friend"

" Who Kate?"

" Yes her"

" She is acting like your best friend Cam"

" What do you mean.."

" Cameryn, she is a..

" A what?"

" This is going to be very hard to show you"

" Look Cam, watch this video, i took at her house.

I watch the video. She was talking about how she was planning to take me out to her parents.

" It is true.. Oh my gosh"

I started to cry. I did not know what to think. I was so confused, and scared. I did not

what to do.

" It is okay".

After Jozie left, I went straight downstairs to tell my Aunt Alyssa and Uncle John about what just happened to me. When I went down stairs they were watching the Originals, I guess they did not watch it on Thursday night. But anyways, I sat next to Aunt Alyssa.

Chapter 6

When I get home my aunt is staring at the tv. “Whats going on aunt Alyssa”. I said

“Look Cameryn, you’re on tv” she says.

“Why are my hands heallng him!” I say

“Their your powers, Cam”

“Powers? That's not true there is no such thing.”

“Yes their is Cameryn, your mom and dad both had powers”

“Huh. How is this even possible?”

“Cam I want you to listen to me, you may not believe me but just listen, please. You are not from earth. You are from a Planet called Galaxis. Spectralmask took over your planet when you were 6 years olds. Your parents died from them. They are looking for people from Galaxis. They are trying to find you (and people like you) so they can take your powers and kill you. That's how your mom and dad died. They were not strong enough to kill them. I promised your mom that i wouldn't tell you until your powers started to develop. This will take awhile, about of month just to get powers all developed. I know you probably have lots more questions, but just go to bed now and we will talk about it in the morning. Uncle John and I need to find a way to delete this off the internet."

" Okay " I said. I walked up stairs to my room and pulled out my computer. I was trying to search for things, that were related to the powers i have, but there was nothing. I couldn't sleep that night. I was still so surprised about the whole thing. Im still not sure if i believed it. Then A girl named jozie showed up in my room!

"Umm, who are you?" I said

" My name is Jozie. I need to tell you important stuff. Ok? Just listen." She said.

Jozie started to tell me about my past and what happened and how kate was after me. I was very worried that kate was going to try to kill me. Jozie told me that she was one of the most powerful people here. I needed to tell aunt Alyssa about my dream. Also, surely she knew what to do. I was going to watch netflix with my best friend Kate. She was going to come over tonight. I needed to find away to tell her now. We usually talk about things and eat our favorite ice cream. I have told Kate about everything. All my powers and the people coming for me. She knows about all my weaknesses and things i can do. I have trusted Kate all these years, but know i know it was all fake. That is why it has been so weird talking to her, she has been wanting to know everything i know. I knew i should've stopped talking about it when she was asking me. This was still all new to me to. I am very scared now. She had been lying to me all this time about who she really is. I still couldn't sleep so i decided to go to starbucks. I grabbed my wallet and went out my window. Starbucks was about to close, but I made it their just in time. I ordered my drink and payed. I waited there for a few minutes and started walking home.

While i was walking home something strange started happening . My hands started to tingle and the next thing i know i'm holding a car up with my hand. I started to run. It dint even burn me when the coffee flew all over me.But then i started to go invisible too.I kept going in and out of invisibility. Great. Another one of my powers. I needed to get home fast, to Aunt Alyssa.

Chapter 7

I finally made it back home. I told aunt Alyssa everything. She said don't worry about and just go get some sleep you have school tomorrow. My head was pounding then i had a flashback of me first getting my pow

I woke up around 7 that morning because i had school. I really did not want to go. I was scared I would see all the Juniors I saw yesterday. I went into my bathroom and took off my coffee stained shirt because i dint feel like changing and took a hot shower. I washed all the salt water, and sand out of my hair from yesterday. I got out of my warm shower and grabbed my towels so i could dry off. I went back into my room and sat in front of my big mirror and blowed dryed my hair. Today was Friday. So i was going to invite Kate over, like what we usually do every Friday. Once I finished my blow drying my hair I plugged my straightener in and straightened my hair. I just left my hair flow down my back. I put on some mascara, blush and some nude lipstick and called it a day. I put on my victoria secret pink shirts with some skinny jeans. I put on white converse and go downstairs to the kitchen.

I get some greek yogurt and put some strawberries and raspberries and blackberries. I grab a spoon from the draw and sit at the table. I look throw my Instagram feed and look to see if anybody's said anything. Im very surprised, but i don't see anything about the shark attack our about me saving Brad's life. It was about 9:00 a.m. when I finished. School started at 10:00. I decided to work on my projects and homework. I finish my math homework and one page of an essay. It was now 9:30. I usually left around 9:45. But since i had nothing to really do I grabbed my backpack and all of my text books and left. When i got there, I saw the surfer guys.

Once I parked i tried to ignore them as much as I could. But I couldn't. They walked right beside me where i was walking. One of them says "Hi Camryn"

"Hi" I say.

" Incase you didn't know i'm Micah and this is Luke and Brad and Ty" Said Micah.

" Oh well hi everyone. Why are you guys by me?" I say

" Well, because you have some sort of powers, You saved my life." Says Brad

" I don't have powers" I mumbled.

" Okay, whatever you say Cam" Said Luke.

" Um, ok.." I say

" Oh sorry, is it okay if i call you that?"

" Sure, I guess." I say.

" Okay well see you around. You should come surfing again today after school." Says brad

" Maybe" I say.

The bell rings and i walk to my locker and open it up. I put the stuff i don't need into my locker and head to English class. I walked into it like I would any other day. I didn't notice anybody, starting or looking at me. Mrs. Sunny started teaching her lesson over Punctuation.I leaned on my forearm and my eyes closed. The next thing I know, the bell rings and it is time for 2nd, science...

I skip through school really fast. I'm still thinking about if i should go surfing. It was a bit cloudy today, I think it was going to rain and I have homework and Kate and I got to hang out too. When i was driving home, I stopped at the stop light and that whole squad of boys pulled up. I tried to look away but they were calling my name.

" Oh. Hi guys" I said

"Hey cam!" said Ty

" So, what you guys doing?"

“ Going to go surf after we change, you coming?” said Luke

“ Uhh, I don't know” I said

“ Please come. Everybody says the waves our great today because of the storm coming! Hurry so we can get done before the storm Cam!” Said Brad.

“ Okay maybe” I said.

The light turns green before I knew it. I guess I would come with them for a little. How bad could it be?

I went home and grabbed my stuff for another day at the beach. but instead of having to grab anything. I was trying to see if i had another one of my powers and i did. I was able to lift things up without even grabbing anything with my hands. It floated up. I pulled it close to me and it worked! I was able to do everything, without touching it. Just using my powers. Kate texted me and said she was going out to dinner tonight with Josh, her boy friend. She invited me to come to. She said she would pick me up at 7:30. I agreed and

went up stairs and slipped on my wetsuit. I put my hair into a messy bun and I went downstairs and decided to make myself something to eat. I decided to make myself a sandwich with some strawberries on the side and without using any of my powers. I opened the pantry and took out the bread. Then, i opened the fridge with a soft swift and took out ham and cheese with the strawberries on the side. I forgot i needed to take off my make up to so I walked upstairs and took it off.

Once i was ready to leave, I opened the door and called for lucky to come to. I grabbed my surfboard and the leash for lucky. Lucky came running. I lifted her up with my powers and put her in the car. I plugged my phone in with the AUX cord because it was almost dead and listened to some music on my way to the beach.

When i got there the whole squad full of boys were already there, out in the ocean surfing the waves. I found a spot to lay down my stuff and got the ball for lucky and threw it into the blue, deep waters of the ocean. I got my surfboard and went into the ocean. I went over to where the squad of boys were hanging out.

" Hey guys!" I said.

" Oh hey Cam, I din't think you were going to come today" Said brad.

"Well I came, so ready to catch some waves today?" I said.

" Ya" Said Luke.

Lucky came swimming by me so i could throw the ball. I picked up the ball, making sure i actually used my hands this time and threw it closer to shore this time.

“ Is that your dog?” Said Ty

“ Ya, her name is Lucky” I said.

We must of all seen the big wave coming because we all layed down on our boards.

“ I bet you Brad will be the first one to wipe out” Ty said.

“ Ya maybe, but for sure i will be the last to wipe out” I said with some sass and a grin on my face.

We all stood up on our board and surfed the wave. Brad was the first one to wipe out. This one curved around and I got out of the tunnel, Everyone else wiped out. I finally wiped out, and everybody was clapping for me and cheering for me. I don't know why though, I have done that before. The squad of boys came over.

" Hi Cam. What is up?" She said

"Well you are never going to believe what just happened to me, a little while ago," I said. Uncle John Paused the show. "What happened Cam," He said worriedly.

"So tJozie appeared in my room.Jozie showed me a video of

Kate talking to her parents (Spectralsk) about new things about me she learned and how they were going to destroy me!" I said.

"Oh... My gosh Cam", Aunt Alyssa said.

"I know, I do not know what to do" I said.

"Well you have to kill her and her parents, and get rid of all their evidence of you being from Galaxis" Uncle John said.

"But she is my best friend, i can not just kill her" I said

" No, she is not your best friend. She is an enemy out to kill you" Aunt Alyssa said.

"Okay, but when" I said.

" Not now, but soon. Just go to bed now" She said. I walked back upstairs, with a trail of thoughts still lurking behind me. I slipped into my bed covering the sheets over me. I grabbed my phone and plugged it in. I went threw my Instagram feed and my twitter feed.i decided to tweet something. I said "Confused. Hurt. Confused." Then after 5 minutes have passed, I fell asleep.

I woke up around 9 a.m. I scrolled through my twitter feed. 71 retweets. Not bad. I went on Instagram to see if anything was new. I also decided to post a photo, I went threw my camera roll and found a picture of me

And Lucky. My caption was Live love Dogs and put the little dog emoji□ and hit post.

Surprisingly my first like was Micah. I decided today that I was going to go shopping. I went over to my dresser and got some plain denim shorts out. I slipped on a black halter then a maroon cardigan. I went sat at my vanity and took out my makeup and hair stuff and put on some mascara and blush and since my hair is naturally wavy, I straightened it, and took some pieces of my hair and did a french braid and pinned it back onto my hair. I decided I did not really like my outfit choice so instead of the maroon cardigan i just took it off and wore the black halter. I put on some white sandals, and brushed my teeth. I walked down stairs and Aunt Alyssa was sitting there drinking some coffee watching TV.

"I'm going out shopping, I will be back soon then i can practice my powers.Ok?" I said

"Ok Cam.See you later then"

I decided to bring Lucky because it was an outdoor shopping center. My phone dinged and I saw I got a text from Kate. It said "Hey Cam, I was wondering if you wanted to hang out"

I just ignored it and got in my car. I started to head for the shopping center. When i got there I went into Pink and bought me some tank tops and new leggings. Since it was around lunchtime I headed over to Chipotle. I got myself a bowl and sat outside so Lucky could be with me too. When I sat down I notice Micah was standing in line at Chipotle, He saw me and I smiled and waved at him. I snapchatted my chipotle and put it on my story. I saw Micah start to walk over to me.

“Hey Micah!”

“Hi Cam, did not expect you to be here. What's up?”

“Nothing much. How about you?”

“Well i am having lunch with a pretty girl” He said with a smirk”

“You are funny. But thanks I guess.”

“Ya”

“I noticed that you were my first like on my post”

“Yup. So what are you doing later.”

“I have to work on some stuff with my Aunt.”

“Oh, well what are you doing after lunch?”

“Going back shopping with Lucky”

“Mind if i join you guys”

“No not at all, you can come.”

“Alright, thanks”

“No problem. Do you need me to drive you?”

“Um sure if you want.”

“Ok”

I got up and we all walked over to my car. I had to put Lucky in the back because Micah was sitting in the front. I have not hung out with a boy like this in a while. The last time was with my ex, Cole. We did not speak to each other on the way there. We were both kind of shy I guess. When we got there we walked over to the Nike factory.

We went over to the shoes section

We walked in and went over to the shoe part of the store.

" What kind of nike shoes are you looking for?" I said

" Maybe some Roches"

" Same I need some new shoes" He said.

I went over to the women's sections, I looked for some Roches and the only ones they had was some peach ones that I really liked. I grabbed a my size, a 8 and went over to Micah.

" What do you think of these"

"Those are nice! I love the black, they look fresh"

"Thanks. What color did you get?"

" I got peach"

"Nice."

"Thanks."

We both walked over to the checkout counter. I paid for mine and he paid for his. We both decided to get some Ice Cream.

Chapter 8

Around 4:00 I drove him back to Chipotle and we went our separate ways. I drove home with Lucky hanging her head out the window, with her big tongue dangling from her mouth. I pulled into my driveway and parked my car. I took Lucky and we walked inside with my bags, that I got shopping today.

"Hey Aunt Alyssa"

"Hi Cam, good shopping day?"

" Ya, I got some good stuff"

"Good, ready to practice?'

"Ya

I changed my clothes into some shorts and a tee-shirt with my new Roches on and headed out to practice with my Aunt Alyssa. The flashback just came back again...I'm trying to think why this keeps happening to.

-- We walked in and went over to the shoe part of the store.

" What kind of nike shoes are you looking for?" I said

" Maybe some Roches"

" Same I need some new shoes" He said.

I went over to the women's sections, I looked for some Roches and the only ones they had was some peach ones that I really liked. I grabbed a my size, a 8 and went over to Micah.

" What do you think of these"

"Those are nice! I love the black, they look fresh"

"Thanks. What color did you get?"

" I got peach"

"Nice."

"Thanks."

We both walked over to the checkout counter. I paid for mine and he paid for his. We both decided to get some Ice Cream.

Around 4:00 I drove him back to Chipotle and we went our separate ways. I drove home with Lucky hanging her head out the window, with her big tongue dangling from her mouth. I pulled into my driveway and parked my car. I took Lucky and we walked inside with my bags, that I got shopping today.--

"Hey Aunt Alyssa"

"Hi Cam, good shopping day?"

" Ya, I got some good stuff"

"Good, ready to practice?'

"Ya

I walked outside with Aunt Alyssa and Lucky.

“Okay. So this is also going t sound very crazy. BUt Lucky is a superdog.” SHe said.

“ A superdog?”

“ Yes, she has powers where she can change into huge beast and other animals to fight off Spectralsk. She can help you Cam!”

“ Well, that's great. I will need so much help as i need.”

“ And, Jozie came by. She was in our room last night with me and Uncle John.”

“ Oh. What did she say?”

“ She said Kate and her family were planning an attack on you. SO you have to be prepared. Jozie said she is going to help you if they come. Jozie is also going to find lots of people to help you kill them because they are the most powerful people in the world.”

“ Oh well, that is even better!”

“ Yes. So let us get practicing” She said.

“ Ok”

“ So first i want you to run from the the fence all the way down to the other fence. I am going to test your speed.”

“ Um ok”

I walked over to the fence. I was never really that fast at running. I thought just maybe i will be able to have another power. Maybe i could run fast..

" Okay, are you ready?"

" Ya"

" Ready. Set. GO!"

I ran as fast I could to the other side of the fence. I finally got their.

" .35 seconds. Cam thats fast."

" Oh my gosh. I did not know i could run that fast."

" Ya neither did I, that is the fastest ever. Faster than you run to the fridge when you are hungry!"" She said laughing.

" Ya true." I also said laughing.

"Okay. Next I want you to turn invisible. Then go inside grab us some waters. Then come back!"

" Okay, I will try.."

I stand there for a few minutes and try to go invisible. But i am not trying hard enough. I think really hard to turn myself invisible and it works. I go inside and grab some ice cold waters. Then I go back outside.

"Nice Cam!"

I make myself un invisible.

“Thanks Aunt Alyssa.”

“ Okay, next I need you to try and make a force field around, Lucky and me and you.” She said

“ Okay. I have never tried this before.”

“Well since you have invisibility you should be able to make a force field as well” She said

“ Umm. Okay I guess.”

I thought really hard in my mind to make myself do a force field. Then all of the sudden it worked. It was like this shield around us.

Chapter 9

" Good job Cam you are doing it! Try to hold it for at least 10 more seconds!" She said really happily

I think I held it for at least 20 more seconds. It really tired me out doing that.

" Oh wow. I did it. " I said out of breath still.

" Yes you did Cam! Know the last one for today. I am going to give myself a cut and I need you to heal it" She said.

" Okay if you say so"

Aunt Alyssa walked inside the house and got a knife. She walked about outside like she was really nervous. She took the knife and cut herself on the arm. I walked over and grabbed her arm. I placed my hand on her and the cut started to heal itself. I did it. I healed someone again!

" Oh my gosh Cam. You did it!"

"Thank you. I am going to take a shower now ok?" I said

" Ya sure Cam!"

I was really exhausted after that. I went upstairs into my room and I saw Jozie sitting there on my bed.

" Hi Jozie. What is up?"

" I have to tell you something about Kate."

“ Ok”

“ She is planning to attack you tomorrow. You have to be prepared” She said.

“ I think I am. I was practicing for like 2 hours just now.”

“ Good. Just be ready. Okay Cam?”

“ Okay Jozie!”

She disappeared like that and I went to take a shower. After my shower, I put on my PJ’s and called it a night. In the morning I will tell Aunt Alyssa about what Jozie said, unless Jozie already told her about it.

Chapter 10

I woke up around 9:00 today because all i could think about was how Kate and her family were going to try to kill me today. Still in my pj’s I walked down stairs to tell Aunt Alyssa and Uncle John about it. When I walked down they were no place to be seen. Lucky was down stairs whimpering like something was wrong. I walked up to Lucky and started to pet her.

“ What is wrong Lucky girl?”

She just kept on whimpering. I tried to call Aunt Alyssa and Uncle John but they did not answer my call. I started to call Jozie's name,

"Jozie, I need your help. Where is Aunt Alyssa and Uncle john?"

I said it about a few times. No response. After I said it a few more times, Jozie appread.

"Cam"

"Ya.."

" Kate and her family have Aunt Alyssa and Uncle John. You have to go there right now and fight them both."

" How i'm not ready. Jozie. I am really scared..."

" It is okay. I have contacted people just like you. Who came from Galaxis. Plus, I will be helping you too Cam. We got this."

" I guess"

My phone started to ding. I got a text from Micah.

Micah: I am coming Cam. Do not worry.

Me: What do you mean?

Micah: I have powers. Just like you.

Me: Wait. What.

Micah: I am from the planet Galaxis. Just like you. Jozie your mentor contacted me and told me everything.

Me: Ok I guess. Come to my house. We can drive over there together.

Micah: Ya. I am on my way.

I got dressed really quick. I Just put on some leggings and a peach shirt with my new peach roshe's too. I left my hair down and put on foundation and mascara and lightly applied some blush to my cheeks. By the time I was finished Micah knocked my door of my house. I called Lucky to come because I knew she could help too.

" Hi"

" Hi Cam, like your shoes."

" Thanks." I noticed he was wearing his too" " I like your shoes too"

"Thanks. We should get going"

We walked over to his car. I put Lucky in the back of his car.

" Is it okay that she is back there?"

" Ya that fine."

" Ok thank you. Lucky is not a dog. She turns into a huge beast. I think Kate's dog is like Lucky too."

" Ya. I should've brought my dog if I would of knew too. I bet mine would turn into a beast too."

" So. When did you find about all of this?"

" I found out about 3 years ago. I have never seen a Spectrlask before. So I don't really know how this is going to work."

" Me too. I found out the day I healed Brad at the beach. My Aunt told me everything. What kind of powers do you have?" I asked him.

" I am really strong. I can talk to animals I also can run really fast and read people's mind."

"Oh. Nice." I said.

Chapter 11

We pulled up at Kate's house. I got lucky out of the car. Micah and I walked up to the door. Micah kicked the door right open.

" AUNT ALYSSA. UNCLE JOHN. WHERE ARE YOU" I scream really loud.

" Oh hi Cam. Glad to see you showed up." Said Kate.

" How could you do this Kate?"

I turned invisible without hearing another word. I saw Kate's mom and her dad. They did not look like humans. They had bright red eyes. They also had like five rows of teeth. There teeth looked razor sharp. Like they could cut through anything. Still invisible I saw Micah talking to Kate. I grabbed his hand and he went invisible too.

" Micah"

" Ya Cam?"

I pulled him where is mom and dad were standing.

" Look we have to kill them first."

" Ok"

Me and Micah both turned un invisible. I went for Kate's mom first and Micah went for Kate's dad.

" Oh look who decided to show up" Kate's mom said.

" Mmm"

Then I had my gun I had in my back pocket. I pulled it out and shot at her right in the face. She doged.

" I do not know why you try Cam baby. We will win, you have no chance."

"Mmm"

Kate's mom pulled out one of there weapons. Oh no. I had nothing compared like that. I had to get it from her. I shot another bullet at her. It went into her stomach but nothing happend. She started to come close to me, were she could be able to hit me with the sword looking thing. The took a swing but I went invisible and ran. I ran over to where Micah was fighting. He was all bloody and on the ground. I took at my gun and shot the Spectrask right in the head. I saw one of the weapons on the floor and picked it up. I stabbed it right in his head and he fell to the ground. In about thirty seconds he turned to ash and disappeared. Isaw Kate coming. But she could not see me. She was walking over to Micah with a fireball thing coming out of her hand. She raised to her hand up to strike him. But as she was throwing it, I jumped in front of him and put a force field around him.

"Thanks"

Kate got so angry with that. I got her I told him you find her mom and fight her off. But something caught my eye. In the backyard was Lucky as a huge beast and so was Kate's dog sammy. The were fighting. But lucky of course was kicking Sammy's booty.

I turned back to Kate and gave her a smirk. With one of the swords in my hand I stood up. Kate tried to throw this thing at me. but I grabbed it in mid air and turned it and threw it at her. It striked it right in her heart. I walked up to her.

" I am sorry Kate"

I took the sword and stabbed her right in the head

" Cam" Kate said. Then she disappeared. I walked over to where Micah was fighting. Micah was winning this one. Even though he probably did not need help I stabbed Kate's mom right in the head.

" I think it is over" I said. She shook her head no.

" Micah go find my Aunt Alyssa and Uncle John. Please"

" Yes. Of course"

I walked back outside where Lucky and Sammy was fighting. Sammy was on the ground. Dead. Lucky won. I knew my girl would. I saw Lucky had some scratches on her. Lucky turned back to her regular size. I placed my hands on her side and they healed instantly. Me and Lucky walked back into the house.

Micah was there with my Aunt Alyssa and Uncle John. I started bawling crying right when I saw them. They both looked like they have been beaten up too.

" Oh my gosh" I said in between tears. I touched all their cuts to heal them.

" I am so thankful for you Cam. I love you so much" said Aunt Alyssa

" WE love you so much" said Uncle John. We all walked out the house. Then I fainted. My head was spinning around and around i couldn't see anything. I had another flashback. Summer break was over. It was my sophomore year at West Coast high School. My name is Camryn Blu. I Live in California. I have light brown hair (almost blonde), green eyes and very tan. I have lived in Cali for about 2 years. I'm originally from NY city . My mom and dad both died when i was only 7 year old. I never knew why. I have alway lived with my aunt Alyssa and My uncle John. My best friend is Kate. Im sitting in Social studies. I've always hated that class. When i get home i'm going to go to go surfing. The bell finally rings and i got to my advanced math class with all the nerds. I got put into this class because i catch along quick and everything is just easy to me. I've always really liked school too. I start to copy the notes in my journal about the new math material we are learning. The bell rings and i got to my locker and grab my stuff. I grab my backpack and all my books to go home.

After school i went straight home. I found my wet suit and pulled my hair into a dutch braid and took off all my makeup, so i did not look like a zombie while i was surfing the waves. I would invite Kate but she is really scared of sharks or she is scared she will die. I decide to bring Lucky because she loves the water. Belmont Shore, is a dog friendly place. The beach is about a 10 minute ride from my house. I get in my jeep, and turn on the bluetooth and start to sing to .

The next thing I know i'm at Belmont Shore. I get my surfboard and let lucky out the car.

I walk over to spot where I lay my bag and towel down onto the sand. I grab lucky's ball and throw it into the water for her to fetch. I get my surfboard and walk over the the water. I step in WIth my black wetsuit and swim out to wait for a wave. There was a lot of surfers out here today. I have never seen a shark attack or even seen a shark before, so i'm not scared of anything. I wait for a good wave. Finally one comes, I get on my stomach and wait for it to come. Right while it is pushing me i stand up on my board. I love the beachy air and water splashing in my face, this is what i live for.

I finally wipe out and go back out for another wave. Some guys were all hanging out around that area too. We all talking and waiting for a wave to come. " So what school do you go to?" asked one of the guys. " I got to west coast high" I said. There was a moment of silence. Then the next thing i heard was a scream from one of the boys. I look over and he is pulled under the water. The only thing that came to mind was shark. I had to get out of there, but I couldn't just leave him. I swam over to where is surfboard lays. I grab what is left of his arm, as he comes to the surface of the water.

I pull him onto my surfboard. I see the shark coming, so i kick it into the nose and it swims away.

I walk over to spot where I lay my bag and towel down onto the sand. I tell someone to call 911. I lay him down. He is screaming and crying. I put my arm on the his stomach where is was also bitten. I try to stop the blood, but it stops on its own. My hands. They are healing him... I get up and run. I don't know what to do. My hands were healing him. I don't know how. It just closed up the wounds and stopped the bleeding. I call for lucky, and she comes running. I open the door for her and close it. I get in my jeep and go straight home.

Chapter 13

When I get home my aunt is staring at the tv. “Whats going on aunt Alyssa”. I said

“Look Cameryn, you’re on tv” she says.

“Why are my hands healIng him!” I say

“Their your powers, Cam”

“Powers? That's not true there is no such thing.”

“Yes their is Cameryn, your mom and dad both had powers”

“Huh. How is this even possible?”

“Cam I want you to listen to me, you may not believe me but just listen, please. You are not from earth. You are from a Planet called Galaxis. Spectralmask took over your planet when you were 6 years olds. Your parents died from them. They are looking for people from Galaxis. They are trying to find you (and people like you) so they can take your powers and kill you. That's how your mom and dad died. They were not strong enough to kill them. I promised your mom that i wouldn't tell you until your powers started to develop. This will take awhile, about of month just to get powers all developed. I know you probably have lots more questions, but just go to bed now and we will talk about it in the morning. Uncle John and I need to find a way to delete this off the internet."

" Okay " I said. I walked up stairs to my room and pulled out my computer. I was trying to search for things, that were related to the powers i have, but there was nothing. I couldn't sleep that night. I was still so surprised about the whole thing. Im still not sure if i believed it. Then A girl named jozie showed up in my room!

"Umm, who are you?" I said

" My name is Jozie. I need to tell you important stuff. Ok? Just listen." She said.

Jozie started to tell me about my past and what happened and how kate was after me. I was very worried that kate was going to try to kill me. Jozie told me that she was one of the most powerful people here. I needed to tell aunt Alyssa about my dream. Also, surely she knew what to do. I was going to watch netflix with my best friend Kate. She was going to come over tonight. I needed to find away to tell her now. We usually talk about things and eat our favorite ice cream. I have told Kate about everything. All my powers and the people coming for me. She knows about all my weaknesses and things i can do. I have trusted Kate all these years, but know i know it was all fake. That is why it has been so weird talking to her, she has been wanting to know everything i know. I knew i should've stopped talking about it when she was asking me. This was still all new to me to. I am very scared now. She had been lying to me all this time about who she really is. I still couldn't sleep so i decided to go to starbucks. I grabbed my wallet and went out my window. Starbucks was about to close, but I made it their just in time. I ordered my drink and payed. I waited there for a few minutes and started walking home.

While i was walking home something strange started happening . My hands started to tingle and the next thing i know i'm holding a car up with my hand. I started to run. It dint even burn me when the coffee flew all over me.But then i started to go invisible too.I kept going in and out of invisibility. Great. Another one of my powers. I needed to get home fast, to Aunt Alyssa.

I finally made it back home. I told aunt Alyssa everything. She said don't worry about and just go get some sleep you have school tomorrow. My head was pounding then i had a flashback of me first getting my pow

I woke up around 7 that morning because i had school. I really did not want to go. I was scared I would see all the Juniors

I saw yesterday. I went into my bathroom and took off my coffee stained shirt because i dint feel like changing and took a hot shower. I washed all the salt water, and sand out of my hair from yesterday. I got out of my warm shower and grabbed my towels so i could dry off. I went back into my room and sat in front of my big mirror and blowed dryed my hair. Today was Friday. So i was going to invite Kate over, like what we usually do every Friday. Once I finished my blow drying my hair i plugged my straightener in and straightened my hair. I just left my hair flow down my back. I put on some mascara, blush and some nude lipstick and called it a day. I put on my victoria secret pink shirts with some skinny jeans. I put on white converse and go downstairs to the kitchen.

I get some greek yogurt and put some strawberries and raspberries and blackberries. I grab a spoon from the draw and sit at the table. I look throw my Instagram feed and look to see if anybody's said anything. Im very surprised, but i don't see anything about the shark attack our about me saving Brad's life. It was about 9:00 a.m. when I finished. School started at 10:00. I decided to work on my projects and homework. I finish my math homework and one page of an essay. It was now 9:30. I usually left around 9:45. But since i had nothing to really do I grabbed my backpack and all of my text books and left. When i got there, I saw the surfer guys.

Once I parked i tried to ignore them as much as I could. But I couldn't. They walked right beside me where i was walking. One of them says “Hi Camryn”

“Hi” I say.

“ Incase you didn't know i’m Micah and this is Luke and Brad and Ty” Said Micah.

“ Oh well hi everyone. Why are you guys by me?” I say

“ Well, because you have some sort of powers, You saved my life.” Says Brad

“ I don't have powers” I mumbled.

“ Okay, whatever you say Cam” Said Luke.

“ Um, ok..” I say

“ Oh sorry, is it okay if i call you that?”

“ Sure, I guess.” I say.

“ Okay well see you around. You should come surfing again today after school.” Says brad

“ Maybe” I say.

The bell rings and i walk to my locker and open it up. I put the stuff i don't need into my locker and head to English class. I walked into it like I would any other day. I didn't notice anybody, starting or looking at me. Mrs. Sunny started teaching her lesson over Punctuation.I leaned on my forearm and my eyes closed. The next thing I know, the bell rings and it is time for 2nd, science...

I skip through school really fast. I'm still thinking about if i should go surfing. It was a bit cloudy today, I think it was going to rain and I have homework and Kate and I got to hang out too. When i was driving home, I stopped at the stop light and that whole squad of boys pulled up. I tried to look away but they were calling my name.

" Oh. Hi guys" I said

"Hey cam!" said Ty

" So, what you guys doing?"

" Going to go surf after we change, you coming?" said Luke

After that long flashback i realized something. Everytime im having these flashbacks i notice something... im seeing people ive seen before. Like my mom and my dad. I just saw them during my flashback they were helping me save Brad they had laid their hands on his arm just like i did. And during when i was healing Aunt Alyssa and Uncle John.

Micah drove us all home. None of us said a word the whole ride home either. We went into our house. I told Micah he could stay if he wanted too but he went home. . Aunt Alyssa told me later that Jozie was really my mom. She was helping this whole time during my journey. I just never realized it or saw her. I was in disbelief, i would of never guess that jozie, my mentor, who looked 18 was my mom. I'm really thankful that she was their. Giving me advice along the way. Without her help i would've end up dead, so would Aunt Alyssa and Uncle John.

I guess being from Galaxis wasn't bad after all. I had powers like nobody else, well except Micah. I was really thankful for my mom(Jozie) because without her, i would of been dead... Me and Micah hang out alot. I still go surfing with all those boys. Micah got a new power too. He brainwashed everyone at our school that we did not have powers. So that was good. Everyone is happy here in Beverly hills.

Few weeks later.

I walked upstairs and I took a quick shower and got on some clean clothes. I walked back down stairs and sat on the couch next to Aunt Alyssa.

" Hey cam"

" Hi, what are you watching?"

" Just watching the Cooking Channel , but i need to tell you something."   "Ya, what is it?"

"Well We are moving" Aunt Alyssa said.

" What" I said.

" I know I don't want to move either. But we have too." She said.

"What why..." I said.

" Because Cam, they know we are here, we have to be safe and go some where else." She said

" No, but what about Micah, and all my friends!"

" Micah, will be coming with us." She said with a smile

" Really." I said more exicedlty"

" Ya me and his

PREVIEW OF NEXT STORY: there's more out their. I have moved back to New york. Aunt Alyssa told me it wasn't safe there anymore. Micah is with us too. I know they are following us, and at our new school. I'm pretty sure somebody is a Galaxis. Her name is Lace. Also Uncle John has bought a new dog. It's a puppy. He is just like Lucky. His name is Rocky(a husky). They will have to fight off more Specktralsk to try to save the city, because Spectralsk are trying to take over the world.

www.ingramcontent.com/pod-product-compliance
Ingram Content Group UK Ltd.
Pitfield, Milton Keynes, MK11 3LW, UK
UKHW041919190726
13854UKWH00003B/1338

9 781365 023606